THE
BLAMMO-SURPRISE!
BOOK

A Story to Help Children Overcome Fears

By Stephen R. Lankton

Illustrated by Nancy Wiley

Magination Press
A Division of Brunner/Mazel, Inc.
New York

Library of Congress Cataloging-in-Publication Data

Lankton, Stephen R.
  The blammo—surprise! book.

  Summary: Knowsis uses his Blammo-Surprise! Book
to help Terry conquer her fear of the circus through her
own thinking and imagination.
  [1. Fear—Fiction. 2. Circus—Fiction] I. Wiley,
Nancy, 1964–   ill. II. Title.
PZ7.L2774B1   1988   [E]   88-13566
ISBN 0-945354-11-8
ISBN 0-945354-10-X (pbk.)

Copyright © 1988 by Stephen R. Lankton

Published by
Magination Press
An Imprint of Brunner/Mazel, Inc., 19 Union Square West, New York, NY 10003

Paperback edition distributed to the trade by
Publishers Group West
4065 Hollis St., Emoryville, CA 94608
Telephone 800-982-8319; in CA call collect 415-658-3453

Distributed in Canada by
Book Center
1140 Beaulac St., Montreal, Quebec H4R 1R8, Canada

MANUFACTURED IN THE UNITED STATES OF AMERICA

10 9 8 7 6 5 4 3 2 1

INTRODUCTION FOR PARENTS

All children experience fears. Some are small fears, which pass quickly. Others are large fears, which last a long time. Whatever the kind or causes of the fears, all parents are anxious to help their children overcome their fright and feel better.

This book has been written to help grown-ups help their children. Parents, grandparents, foster parents, stepparents, aunts, uncles, teachers, counselors, and other adults will find this book instructive and useful. Children will find it delightful.

Children, and adults for that matter, identify with stories. They draw upon aspects of their own lives in order to relate to the characters or plot of the story. This book uses this natural process of human thinking to help parents reduce or eliminate their children's fears. The children in this story have their own unique and appealing personalities, but all children will be able to identify with their reactions.

Although this book does not replace the professional family therapist, psychologist, social worker, or child psychiatrist for complex phobic problems, it does provide a clinically sound process for parents to develop strategies of their own to help their children overcome fears.

This book can help children who are frightened in any of many situations. These include fear of crowds, fear of heights, fear of strangers, fear of being away from parents, fear of being alone, fear of small animals, fear of large animals, fear of loud noises, fear of sudden movement, fear of nightmares, fear of the dark, and many more.

The story begins with the description of one child, Terry's, fear of the circus. It continues with a dialogue between two children, Terry and Knowsis, which is meant to arouse and build appropriate feelings and apply them systematically for the elimination of the fear(s). Parents are urged to read this section with conviction and to involve their child in playful identification with the story. Parents can consider the questions asked by the boy, Knowsis, and the arousal of feelings in the child, Terry, to be a conversation between Knowsis and their own child, or between themselves and their child. Repeated reading of the story will reinforce even the weakest participation by the child, and the surprise ending will help the child make the learnings part of his or her own self-concept.

We hope you and your children will find this story not only helpful in solving problems of phobias, large and small, but also entertaining and a lot of fun.

To Shawn and Alicia,
who learned how to
bust their own
bad dreams

This story is about the day Poodgie, Paradora, and their brother, Knowsis, went to the circus with their friend Terry and helped Terry solve a very big problem.

In the beginning, no one even knew there was a problem, especially Paradora, the big sister. She never, ever knew that there were any problems. She was too busy saying, "Everything is wonderful!" And Poodgie was too happy to think of problems. This was the first year she was old enough to go to the circus.

Knowsis was also very excited about the circus, but he wondered what to do before it was time to go. He got out his crayons and started drawing in an empty book. When he finished, he named it *The Blammo—Surprise! Book,* but he didn't show it to anyone.

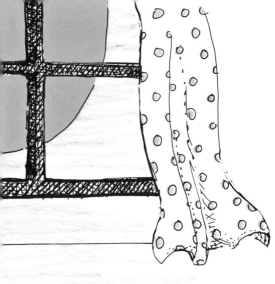

Meanwhile, at her house, Terry
was dreading the trip to the circus.
All week long she had hoped that
the day would never come. But
that Saturday morning the sun
grinned a big hello in her
bedroom window.

It was time to go to the circus. Poodgie, Paradora and Knowsis arrived to walk with Terry across town to where the big tent was set up. Poodgie said she wanted to ride the elephants. She couldn't wait to smell the elephant's thick

grey skin and feel it sway back and forth and hear its feet
go clomp clomp around the ring. She asked Terry if she
would come with her, but she was too excited to listen
to Terry's answer.

As soon as they found their seats, the music started and the clowns ran out. Their faces were painted white with great big smiles. They had curly orange hair and baggy pants and big checkered shirts and suspenders. Poodgie and Paradora and Knowsis giggled as the clowns' shoes flopped on the ground. One clown turned and paddled another clown with a board, and one clown spilled a pitcher of water all over another clown. Poodgie looked over at Terry and said, "Isn't this fun!"

Terry was about as white as the clowns. Poodgie thought she probably liked something better at the circus than the clowns. Paradora was sure she was just waiting for the acrobats. But Knowsis noticed that Terry was holding onto the seat very tightly. He thought she looked a little scared.

He was about to say something when the whistle blew
and the ringmaster threw his hat in the air. The lions came
bounding out of their cages. "Wow!" said Poodgie, "Look at
those big teeth!" "Look at their lovely golden manes," said
Paradora. They all watched as the lion tamer cracked his
whip and made the lions jump through hoops of fire.

Paradora turned around to say to Terry, "Isn't this the greatest circus of all?" Terry had her head down. She wasn't even looking. "What's the matter?" asked Poodgie. "Are you scared, Terry?" asked Knowsis. And Terry said, "Well, yes, a little bit."

Just then the lions ran back
into their cages as fast as they
had run out. And the tumblers came
leaping across the circus ring. Now Terry
had tears in her eyes. Knowsis asked, "Why
are you crying, Terry?" She said, "I'm
afraid when they start jumping
around like that."

The acrobats started climbing up the poles. The trapeze artists started swinging back and forth and grabbing hold of each other. Terry was crying real hard now. "Those people are up so high, flying through the air. Something terrible is going to happen."

"That's silly," said Paradora. "If they fall, they'll fall right into the net." Knowsis said, "That's right. There's no need to be scared." "I am though," said Terry. "I'm *really* scared, and I want to go home."

Poodgie said, "Oh, no, not before we ride the elephants. Come on, Terry." She grabbed Terry's hand and headed toward the ticket booth for the elephant ride.

"I don't want to ride the elephants," Terry cried. "I'm scared and I want to go home." She pulled loose from Poodgie.

Knowsis said, "Terry, come with me. I want to show you something I made today." "Okay," said Terry. Anything that would get her away from the circus was a good idea to her.

Now, Knowsis knew that when he went someplace, even if other people got scared, he usually didn't. He had figured out that the reason he didn't feel scared was because he was always busy feeling something else. He had the idea his surprise book might help Terry feel something else.

While Poodgie and Paradora waited for the tickets for the elephant ride, Knowsis and Terry sat quietly outside the tent. Knowsis handed her his *Blammo — Surprise! Book.* "All you have to do," he said, "is listen to what I say, turn the pages when I tell you, and read the pages when you turn them. Are you ready?" Terry said, "Yes."

"First," said Knowsis, "you have to think. Close your eyes and think of being comfortable someplace. You must have been really comfortable in a lot of places before." Terry remembered that she was comfortable when she visited her grandmother. "Good. That's the idea," said Knowsis. "Think of being comfortable before. As soon as you are feeling comfortable, open the first page of the book and look at it. But don't turn the page until you feel a really good comfortable feeling." Then Knowsis waited.

In just a couple of minutes, Terry said, "I'm feeling pretty comfortable now." So she turned the page, and

There was a great big yellow sun with the word "blammo" on it.

"Don't turn any other pages yet," Knowsis said. "First, think of all the things you would like to be feeling instead of scared."

"Well," Terry said, "I would like to feel brave. I'd like to feel happy. I'd like to feel safe. Sometimes I'd like to feel silly. And sometimes confident. And excited!"

"Good," said Knowsis. "Now remember a time you felt very happy." Terry's face lit up when she remembered a time she felt really happy. Knowsis said, "Now think about what was happening, who was there, and how you felt. When you feel really happy, turn the page."

Terry turned the page, and

There was another big yellow sun. Terry laughed, with a big smile on her face.

"Now," said Knowsis, "remember a time and a place when you felt as brave as you would like to feel now."

When Terry's face changed from smiling to looking brave, Knowsis said, "Turn the page now while you are feeling brave."

Terry turned the page, and

There was the sun looking back. Terry felt very brave, with a big smile on her face.

"Now," said Knowsis, "remember a time when you felt silly." That was easy for Terry. She giggled.

Knowsis said, "Turn the page right away, now that you're silly."

Terry turned the page, and

Terry giggled some more, and even felt brave, with a big smile on her face.

"Now," said Knowsis, "remember a time when you felt really safe."

Terry sighed a big relaxed sigh
and smiled a warm little smile.
"When you feel safe, but not
before, turn the page." Terry
enjoyed that feeling of being
safe.

She turned the page, and

Looking at the sun, Terry felt really safe, and a little silly, and even rather brave, with a big smile on her face.

"Now, you've felt happy, brave, silly, and safe. How about confident or excited?" asked Knowsis.

Terry remembered a time when she had gotten all the answers right in a spelling bee. She couldn't decide whether she was feeling confident or excited, but it sure was a good feeling.

So she turned the page, and

Terry's face shined with confidence and excitement. At the same time she felt safe, and a little silly, and rather brave, with a big smile on her face.

"Now," said Knowsis, "think about the earliest time you can remember being scared. But, instead of being scared, look at the blammo-sunshine picture and feel all the good feelings you feel when you see that picture."

Terry turned the page and looked at the sun. The new feelings of confidence and excitement, the comfortable feeling of being safe, the giggle, and the feeling of being brave all came back, along with a big smile on her face. Terry thought about the earliest time she could remember being scared, but thinking about it didn't make her scared now. She was feeling so many good feelings, even while thinking about that old scary time. "I'm not scared now," said Terry.

"Good," said Knowsis. "Let's do that one more time." "Okay," said Terry. "I'm going to think of another time I was scared." Just as she began to remember feeling scared, she turned the page, and

There was the sunshine. Terry said, "I don't feel scared thinking about that time either."

"Good," said Knowsis. "Now, think about being at the circus, and turn the page just as you do." So Terry started thinking about being at the circus.

Just as that scary feeling started coming, she turned the page, and

Terry laughed. She said, "I'm still not afraid. That's amazing."

"Now," said Knowsis, "think about riding on the elephant." Terry confidently thought about riding on the elephant. She turned the page, and

She smiled and giggled and looked brave and happy.

"Now for a surprise," said Knowsis. "Think about how you are not going to have that scary feeling anymore. Then look at the last page." Terry was sure that the last page was going to be another blammo-sunshine. She started thinking about the future. She said, "Okay, now I'm thinking of a new time when I am not going to be scared."

She turned the page, and

She found a mirror at the end of the book. "Surprise!
It's you!" said Knowsis. There was Terry's own face in the
mirror looking comfortable and happy and brave and silly
and safe and confident and excited.

She said, "What a surprise!" "Yes, it is," Knowsis agreed. He added, "That's *The Blammo—Surprise! Book*." "Thank you very much," said Terry, giving him a big hug.

"Come on, it's not too late to ride the elephant," Knowsis urged. "Okay," said Terry. They ran to join Poodgie and Paradora at the ticket line. As she got up on the elephant to ride around the ring, Terry remembered the face that she saw reflected at the end of *The Blammo—Surprise! Book*. And that's the face that she wore all day long. And that's the face she wore most days after that.

And that's how Poodgie, Paradora, and Knowsis solved
Terry's big problem. Of course, Paradora never even knew
there was a problem. And Poodgie thought that she had
saved the day because it was her idea to buy tickets for the
elephant ride. But Knowsis knows that he and his book
helped Terry to use her own thinking and imagination
to stop feeling scared.